Super Zeroes

Rhiannon Lassiter

OXFORD
UNIVERSITY PRESS

OXFORD
UNIVERSITY PRESS

Great Clarendon Street, Oxford OX2 6DP

Oxford University Press is a department of the University of Oxford.
It furthers the University's objective of excellence in research, scholarship,
and education by publishing worldwide in

Oxford New York

Auckland Cape Town Dar es Salaam Hong Kong Karachi
Kuala Lumpur Madrid Melbourne Mexico City Nairobi
New Delhi Shanghai Taipei Toronto

With offices in

Argentina Austria Brazil Chile Czech Republic France Greece
Guatemala Hungary Italy Japan Poland Portugal Singapore
South Korea Switzerland Thailand Turkey Ukraine Vietnam

Oxford is a registered trade mark of Oxford University Press
in the UK and in certain other countries

British Library Cataloguing in Publication Data
Data available

ISBN-13: 978-0-19-275411-4
ISBN-10: 0-19-275411-4

1 3 5 7 9 10 8 6 4 2

Printed in Great Britain by
Cox & Wyman, Reading, Berks.

For Kellie-Ann Takenaka
'It's all about the subtext, dude!'

Contents

1
Multiplicity

People who lived in Multiplicity said it was the best place to live in the world. Everything about Multiplicity was big or fast or strong. The houses were grand, the streets were clean, and the office buildings were titanium star-scrapers with towers that went up into the bright blue sky.

But, best of all, Multiplicity had its very own super heroes!

Every day the *Multiple Times* had a new story about how Captain Excelsior and his daring band had foiled another sinister scheme or locked up another mutant menace or overcome another rampage of reckless robots. When people looked up at the sky they didn't squint and wonder: 'Is that a bird or a plane?' They waved and cheered and shouted: 'Hurrah for Captain Excelsior and the Hero Squad!'

The super heroes were the official protectors of the city. Multiplicity had its own police force, of course, but they only dealt with the small crimes: burglaries and traffic offences and things like that. Whenever there was a really big problem, like an alien invasion or a doomsday device, the mayor would pick up a bright red phone to call the Hero Squad and get them to sort it out. Whatever the problem, they were always able to handle it.

The leader of the Hero Squad was Captain Excelsior. He was tall and handsome and had piercing grey eyes and gleaming white teeth. He'd been an ordinary man until the day he'd been unlucky enough to visit the city museum. It was the same day as an alien spaceship had landed on it and squashed it flat. Captain Excelsior had been injured and nearly died. But the aliens hadn't actually been invading, they'd only stopped to ask for directions, and before they left they used their advanced alien technology to heal him. Ever since then he'd had incredible powers: he could fly, he could run faster than the speed of sound, he could shoot laser beams from his eyes, and he could hear a whisper in a soundproofed room five miles away. But he only used his powers for good and if someone was in trouble all they had to do was shout: 'Help! Captain Excelsior, save me!' and Excelsior would turn up right away to rescue them.

The second-in-command of the Hero Squad was Princess Power. People said she was the most beautiful woman in the world. She was also very intelligent and even before Captain Excelsior had been given his abilities she'd been defending the city, using all sorts of special machines she'd designed herself. She had a rocket pack, and she carried a golden bow and arrow and a utility belt full of gadgets and gizmos. When she zoomed out of the sky with her golden hair rippling in the wind and her beautiful blue eyes searching for villains, innocent people would confess to crimes, just so she would notice them.

The third member of the Hero Squad was Animo. He came from a mysterious floating island in the Pacific Ocean where everyone was vegetarian and people lived in harmony with the animals. Animo was telepathic: he could speak to birds, insects, mammals, and amphibians in their own languages. Because of that, animals would do whatever he wanted. If he needed to cross a river, a hundred fish would make a bridge for him to walk over; if he needed to climb a cliff, a hundred snakes would knot themselves into a rope for him to climb; and if he needed to fly, a hundred birds would come and lift him up into the air.

Together, the Hero Squad was unstoppable. But, all the same, villains never learned and kept trying to take over the city and defeat the heroes. People in Multiplicity were often late to work because they stopped to watch the Hero Squad swooping down out of nowhere to foil an evil plot—sometimes before it even started—and then give interviews to all the reporters and pose for photos in the newspapers. Living in Multiplicity was exciting! People enjoyed reading about the fiendish plans and daring exploits in the *Multiple Times*, or watching the latest deadly device trying to take over the city . . . as long as it was from a safe distance away.

But not quite everyone who lived in Multiplicity admired the Hero Squad.

Dr D. Void was having a bad day.

Bad was D. Void's reason for being. He was a villain, and not just any common villain either. He was an Arch Villain. He was the one responsible for suggesting sinister schemes, manufacturing menacing mutants, or rows and rows of robots designed to rampage across the city.

He did all this from his lair, in a secret location deep beneath the city. Dr D. Void was very proud of his lair and had spent a lot of time designing it so that it fitted with his idea of what an Arch Villain's lair should look like. It had secret passages and false walls, it had a laboratory packed with devices for taking over the world, it had hundreds of henchmen ready to do whatever the boss commanded, and thousands of television screens from which D. Void could see what was happening anywhere in the city. Right now those television screens were showing something very bad—and not

bad the way D. Void liked it.

Everything had been going so well. Earlier that day, giant tanks driven by D. Void's henchmen had driven out of the secret base and into the city. D. Void had smiled and laughed as the news stations had shown pictures of the tanks rolling over parked cars and knocking down phone boxes, and people panicking and running away to avoid being squashed. The giant tanks had rolled right up to the doors of Multiplicity's biggest jewellery store and blasted open the glass windows and all the jewellery cases. Then they had used massive shovels to pick up rings, bracelets, and necklaces and load them into scoops attached to their roofs.

D. Void had giggled and sniggered as he thought of all the valuable jewellery he was stealing. Building dreadful devices cost money and he had to pay the wages of all his hench-people as well. He was looking forward to getting all that lovely glittery gold and silver and those gems into his hands. He might have to construct an extra large safe to fit it all in. But just as he was doodling a design for a wickedly clever combination lock, the television screens started to show something new . . .

The Hero Squad had arrived. Princess Power touched down in a cloud of pink smoke from her jetpack and the news cameras showed her crossing her arms and shaking her head as she stood outside the jewellery store. Dr D. Void grabbed his remote control and turned the sound up just in time to hear her say, 'You villains just made a big mistake. I'm here to tell you that the shops close early today!'

Dr D. Void ground his teeth. Heroes always

had some kind of smart remark to make like that. It was adding insult to injury the way they treated evil schemes like some sort of a joke. Frantically punching buttons on his computer console he contacted the henchman in the first battle tank.

'What are you waiting for, you idiot?' he yelled. 'Blast her!'

In the first tank the henchman heard D. Void's voice come booming out of the

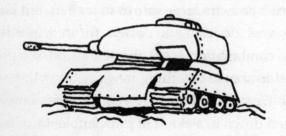

speakers and rolled his eyes. He didn't want to remind the doctor that he'd told them to fire only on his orders. Instead he pulled the levers that would turn the blasting turret around and looked through the periscope to aim the weapon at the princess. He saw her tossing her blonde hair and winking at him, but only for a second. Then Captain Excelsior zoomed up in front of her and his eyes glowed red as he looked at the tank. The henchman slammed his hand down on the fire button and there was a terrible tearing sound and a loud bang. As the inside of the tank filled with smoke, the henchman coughed and choked and fumbled for the door release so that he could escape.

Back in the lab Dr D. Void could see what had happened on his television screens. Captain Excelsior had used his laser vision to weld the gun turret closed, and when it fired it had exploded like a burst banana.

'Don't use the blasters,' the doctor ordered, punching buttons so he could talk to the henchmen in all the other tanks at once. 'Just roll right over them! Crush them like bugs!'

The tanks started to move backwards to where the princess and Captain Excelsior stood but before they reached them, the television screens went black and fuzzy. Dr D. Void reached for the computer console, trying to get rid of the static, but then he realized it wasn't something wrong with the screen. Animo had arrived and with him was a swarm of insects, and not just any insects. They were hornets, the largest, most aggressive type of wasp.

The hornets zoomed up to the tanks and poured through the blasting turrets and into the jewellery scoops, buzzing angrily. After five minutes the doors of the tanks opened and the henchmen came running out, rolling and jumping to try to get away from the stinging insects.

'You cowards, get back in there!' Dr D. Void yelled but his henchmen couldn't hear him. All he could do was pound his fists on the computer console as he watched the Hero Squad taking their bows, as all the people who worked in the shop came out of hiding and cheered.

Then a news reporter appeared on one of the television screens saying, 'Another inspiring victory for the Hero Squad. Stay tuned as we go to an exclusive interview with Captain Excelsior himself.'

Dr D. Void grabbed the remote control and pressed buttons at random to change the channels. Unfortunately he pressed the ones for the Natural World and the Military History channels and all his screens filled up with pictures of wasps and tanks. With a shout of frustration he pulled a blaster out of his pocket and fired at the screens instead. Thirty seconds later he was reeling out of the room, his eyes streaming as he tried to get out of the thick black smoke.

Meanwhile, Captain Excelsior was still taking his bows, Princess Power was posing for photographs, and Animo was giving autographs to anyone brave enough to approach him through the swarm of hornets. A news reporter rushed up to the Hero Squad, with a camera crew following behind her, eager for her exclusive interview.

'Captain, please let me be the first to congratulate you on behalf of the people of Multiplicity on another heroic victory,' she said breathlessly.

'Thank you.' Captain Excelsior beamed at the cameras. 'But I'm only doing my job. I'm just happy we could stop the thieves and save these honest people's business.'

The owner of the jewellery store certainly did

look very grateful; he was kissing Princess Power's hand in thanks. However, the staff looked less happy. They'd realized that they would be the ones who'd have to clean up the broken glass and get all the jewellery out of the wrecked tanks. Cleaning up wasn't hero work.

Sure enough, when they'd finished giving their interviews, the Hero Squad left, waving one last time for the cameras. Animo's hornets had made themselves into a flying carpet, lifting him up into the air to join Captain Excelsior and Princess Power as they flew back to their official headquarters in the Hero Heights skyscraper.

And in a small house on the corner of Excelsior Street and Futurus Avenue, a ten-year-old boy with straight brown hair and scowling brown eyes turned off the TV with a snap. He didn't like super heroes any more than Dr D. Void did and for a very simple reason. Captain Excelsior was his dad.

2
The Invention of Zero

Ben Carter hated his life. His parents were divorced, he didn't have any friends, and he wasn't good at anything. But what Ben hated more than anything else were super heroes.

Everyone else in Ben's class at Bold and Brave Junior School thought super heroes were terrific. They collected Hero Squad stickers and plastic figures and models of Hero Heights and the Hero-Mobile. Even the teachers thought the Hero Squad were great; they set essays and quiz questions about superpowers and the Head told them every day that they should fight evil and protect others, just like the Hero Squad.

Ben got very bad marks at school. All his teachers would sigh and shake their heads and say that Ben was a difficult child. 'He's always so negative about everything,' they complained. 'It's as if he doesn't want to stand out from the crowd at all.' But although some of them noticed that Ben hated talking about super heroes, none of them wondered why.

What people at school didn't know was that Ben's dad was Captain Excelsior. If they had known, he would have been the most popular boy in his class. The teachers would probably have asked for his help making up quizzes for the other kids. People would have stopped him in the street and asked for his autograph.

But Captain Excelsior's real identity was a

secret. Even though everyone knew that Princess Power lived in Power Towers, a huge pink mansion in the north of the city, and that Animo lived in the Menagerie, his own private zoo near the waterfront, no one was supposed to know where Captain Excelsior lived or even his real name.

The thing was that before he'd become a hero Captain Excelsior had been an ordinary person. His name was Keith Carter and he'd lived with his wife and son in a normal house and he'd had a slightly dull job as a health inspector. When he'd discovered that the visiting aliens had given him superpowers he'd immediately wanted to use them to become a hero. But he thought his wife might disapprove. She was a quiet and serious person and she never approved of anything like showing off.

So Keith Carter had sewn himself a costume, secretly, and made a mask to hide his face. When he first went out to find people who needed help, he'd told them he was a new hero named Excelsior and soon he'd been invited firstly to join and then to lead the Hero Squad. He'd enjoyed himself, being on television, flirting with the female reporters, and saving pretty girls and carrying them to safety in his arms. He'd enjoyed it so much that he'd stopped paying much attention to his wife and his baby son and eventually his wife had got so tired of his attention being somewhere else that she'd divorced him.

Keith had never told her he was Captain Excelsior and he'd never told his son either. Ben had worked it out for himself. His mum didn't talk about his father, except for reminding him when it was his weekend for going to Dad's. But, despite what his teachers thought, Ben wasn't stupid. Whenever his dad was late to pick him up, or didn't turn up to something he'd promised to come to, or left Ben alone somewhere because he'd *forgotten something*, Captain Excelsior was always out being brave and noble.

When Ben had first worked it out he'd actually been excited. It was cool to discover your dad was secretly a super hero. But gradually he'd got angrier and angrier about it. His dad obviously cared a lot more about being seen saving the city on television than he did about spending time with Ben. He obviously thought of being a super hero as his real life and Ben as a job that he had to put up with every other weekend.

That was why Ben was the only kid in his class who didn't admire Captain Excelsior. He hated any conversation about superpowers; it just seemed to rub it in that there was nothing special about him.

'In mathematics the most important number is zero. Without zero we wouldn't be able to do maths at all.'

It was the day after the big jewellery store robbery and for the first time all afternoon Ben lifted his head from the desk. Mr Roberts drew a big enthusiastic zero on the board and turned back to the class.

'We use zero all the time without realizing it. Without zero none of the other numbers would count.'

Ben drew a zero in his maths book. It didn't look very important: just a fat round nothing. He thought about telling his mum when

she asked what he learnt in school today:
'Nothing.'

Mr Roberts started writing out sums on the
board, all with zeros in:

$$1 + 10 = ? \quad 1 + 0 = ? \quad 10 - 1 = ?$$
$$0 - 1 = ? \quad 1 \times 10 = ? \quad 1 \times 0 = ?$$
$$10/1 = ? \quad 0/1 = ?$$

Ben drew a smaller circle inside his zero and
turned it into a doughnut. It made him feel
hungry. He copied the sums down and started
trying to work out the answers. The number zero
didn't seem to do much, just sat there and got in
the way.

Ben felt sorry for his doughnut zero and drew
some sprinkles on top of it to make it look more
interesting. He didn't believe Mr Roberts that
zero was special. If you called someone a zero it
meant they were useless, not good at anything.
That morning in games he'd been the last person
picked for a team and one of the other boys had

said, 'I don't see why we have to have Ben on our team. He's such a zero.'

Ben hadn't said anything, just scowled. Then, every time he tried to hit the ball, he'd hit it wrongly and his team had lost and everyone had shouted at him.

Ben hated Fridays. Never being picked for teams and maths lessons about nothing weren't the worst thing. The worst thing about Friday was that every second one his dad was supposed to collect him from school and Ben always had to wait for ages for him to come. By the time Keith Carter's battered old car pulled up outside, everyone else would have left and they'd all have seen him sitting on the kerb waiting.

This weekend Phoenix Park was finally opening. Phoenix Park was a theme park with rollercoasters and a zoo and attractions. It was supposed to have the best rides in Multiplicity and people had been talking all week about how brilliant it was supposed to be. Ben never got to go anywhere special like that. Every time his dad promised to take him somewhere, something went wrong and Keith Carter ran off to change secretly into his Captain Excelsior costume instead.

On his birthday there had been a black cloud of yuck hanging over the city and the Hero Squad had spent all day getting rid of it. When Ben's dad finally showed up at his house, long after the cake had been cut, his excuse was that he'd got caught in traffic. He'd brought Ben an astronaut watch that told the time in fifty different countries and worked under the sea or in space, but Ben refused to wear it.

'You're the one that needs a watch,' he'd said crossly. 'Since you're late for everything.'

Last year Ben's dad was supposed to be coming over for Christmas and he and his mum had waited for hours while the turkey dried up in the oven and the sprouts got all mushy and horrid. Finally they decided to eat without him but the food was so nasty, Ben's mum had ordered pizza instead. They'd eaten it sitting in front of the television, where they saw the mayor on the news congratulating the Hero Squad. Someone had stolen the hundred-foot tall Christmas tree from outside city hall and Captain Excelsior and the others had found it and brought it back. Keith Carter finally showed up with a present for Ben. It was a mobile phone with a video screen so you could see the people who called you, but Ben never used it.

'What's the point?' he said. 'Why should I watch Dad's pathetic excuses as well as hearing them?'

While Ben was daydreaming, Mr Roberts had gone round the class checking everyone's work. When he got to Ben he sighed and reached over to draw crosses over half the answers with a red pen. Then he wrote crossly next to the doughnut, 'This is maths, not art. No doodling in class!'

'Honestly, Ben,' he said. 'I wish just once you'd apply yourself to something. You don't even seem to be trying these days.'

Some of the other children laughed and Mr Roberts frowned at them. It was nearly the end of the day and he went back to his desk to remind everyone to do their homework over the weekend.

'But don't forget to have some fun too,' he said. 'Is anyone doing something exciting?'

'You must be kidding, sir,' one of the other

boys said. 'Everyone's going to Phoenix Park! Even the Head's going!'

Mr Roberts laughed. 'I have to admit I've got a ticket myself. It sounds unmissable. Well, I suppose I'll see you all there. Save me a place on the rollercoaster, OK?'

People grinned and nodded. They liked Mr Roberts. But Ben had looked down at his desk again with a black frown on his face. He knew Mr Roberts hadn't meant anything bad, but he was sick and tired of always being left out.

On the other side of the city, Dr D. Void was working in the lab of his underground lair, putting the finishing touches to his new evil plan. His spies had told him that everyone was going to be at Phoenix Park that weekend and he'd decided it was an excellent place to show off his latest creation.

As he worked, Dr D. Void hummed happily to himself. He always enjoyed building things and imagining the chaos they would wreak on Multiplicity. He had lots of people to help him but now, as he polished the gleaming surface of the laser ports on his new device, he had sent everyone else away so that he could daydream in peace.

Jewel D. Void, the doctor's daughter, had come to tell her father that dinner was nearly ready. But when she realized what he was doing she decided not to disturb him. Walking quietly away she felt almost sorry for him. He always looked forward so happily to each new plan. Even though the Hero Squad managed to beat him every time, he still thought that each new device would be the one that would help him conquer Multiplicity once and for all.

All the same, I wish he wouldn't waste his time on these silly plans, she thought as she walked through the black corridors of the lair. *He ought to realize by now that they're not working*.

Jewel was eleven years old and had long shiny black hair which reached nearly to her waist and bright green eyes which shone whenever she was really interested in something. Jewel went to a girls' private school, where everyone thought she was stuck up because she was driven there and collected each day by a black limousine and she had a glittery diamond bracelet that she had special permission to wear even in games lessons.

After school, the black limousine would take her to a hidden entrance and drive her through secret tunnels beneath Multiplicity back to the underground lair. Inside the lair everything was black; the walls were black, the floors were black, the furniture was black, and the henchmen's uniforms were black. Almost the only things that weren't black were the cats.

Dr D. Void knew that a really menacing villain should give orders while sitting in a black chair and stroking a white angora cat. It said so in *The Villain's Handbook* and *50 Steps Towards World Domination* as well as *Plotting: The Fiendish Way*. So, shortly after setting up the lair, he phoned a pet shop and ordered a hundred angora cats, as white and fluffy as possible. This was so he could be sure that, whatever he was doing, he would have a black chair and a white cat within easy reach. At the time he had congratulated himself on having such a good idea.

Black furniture and white cats do not go well together. The cats clawed long rips in the sofas and made puddles on the floors, they scratched the henchmen, and made strange yowling noises whenever they wanted to be fed. What was even worse was that they left white fur over *everything*. The henchmen were constantly picking it out of the computer equipment, fishing soggy lumps of it out of their mid-morning cups of tea, or brushing it off their black uniforms. They complained about it all the time, except when Dr D. Void could hear. Even Jewel, who liked cats, thought it was a bit much.

Now, as Jewel walked down the corridor of the secret lair she bumped into something suddenly, banging her arm. The space in front of her looked completely empty but a voice from the air said, 'Sorry, Jewel.'

'Oh, it's you.' Jewel looked back at the empty space rubbing her arm crossly. 'I wish you wouldn't keep doing that.'

'Sorry,' the voice said again. 'I didn't see you there.'

'Well, I can't be expected to see you. Honestly,

Fade, if you're going to walk about being invisible you should do it somewhere more sensible.'

The Fade was Dr D. Void's most trusted spy. She could go anywhere and find out anything, because she was invisible. Unfortunately, when she came to make her reports, people often ending up bumping into her and this was the third time it had happened this week. But Jewel liked the Fade more than some of the other villains who worked for her father, even if conversations with her made Jewel feel as if she was talking to herself.

'So what are you doing here anyway?' she asked. 'Did you have something to tell my father?'

'That's right,' the Fade's voice replied, following her. 'I've learnt that Captain Excelsior himself is planning to visit Phoenix Park this weekend.'

'But isn't that where the new evil device is supposed to be launched?' Jewel asked. 'Shouldn't we call that off if Excelsior's going to be there?'

'That's what I thought,' the Fade admitted

and Jewel thought she sounded unhappy. 'But Doctor D. Void thinks this new plan is certain to work. He's not worried at all.'

'Well, he should be!' Jewel stamped her foot and then jumped when an angora cat whose tail she had accidentally trodden on let out an indignant screech.

Jewel bent down to try to console the cat but it hissed at her and ran to take refuge on top of the nearest black sofa, shedding a trail of white fluff as it went.

'It's just stupid,' Jewel went on. 'It's bad enough coming up with such a silly plan in the first place but doing it right under Captain Excelsior's nose is just crazy. Didn't you tell him not to?'

She waited but there was no reply and she realized the Fade had taken advantage of her distraction to slip away. It didn't really surprise her. None of the people who worked for Dr D. Void ever argued with him.

'I'd tell him,' she said to herself, 'but it wouldn't do any good.' She sighed. 'I'd better go and tell Toby,' she decided. 'Maybe he can think of a way to change Dad's mind.'

Toby was Jewel's best friend. He was ten years old and the only other kid who lived in Dr D. Void's secret lair. He was tall for his age and already had muscles, since he was expected to learn karate, judo, and boxing. Like everyone else in the lair he had to wear black but he stood out because his hair was bright red and very spiky.

Toby's father, Terry Tench, was a henchman. Terry's father was a henchman and his grand-father had been a henchman and now, since in modern days things had opened up a bit, his wife was a henchman as well. Terry and Tanya took their jobs seriously and that meant not complaining or criticizing any of the boss's plans, no matter how barmy they seemed to be.

Terry often tried to explain this to his son. He wanted him to be a henchman too when he grew up.

'The boss is always right,' he said. 'That's the first rule of henching. Arch Villains don't like it when people start picking holes in their evil plans.'

But Toby, who almost never saw his parents because they were always working on the next evil plan or villainous scheme or whatever, thought this wasn't fair. He didn't see why people didn't tell Dr D. Void that some of his plans, like the angora cats, just caused a lot of hassle for everyone.

Jewel and Toby always saw the problems with Dr D. Void's evil schemes but no one thought they were important enough to listen to their opinions. Neither of them was expected to know anything about villainy. Henchmen weren't expected to have good ideas and Dr D. Void didn't believe girls could be villains.

'At least not Arch Villains, anyway,' he'd told Jewel. 'You can be a villainess when you're older. Snake Woman or Wasp Girl or something like that. But your mother doesn't want you to wear the kind of clothes villainesses have to until you're at least sixteen.'

'I wouldn't be Wasp Girl if you paid me,' Jewel had said. 'And I don't want to wear those sorts of clothes *ever*. If I can't be an Arch Villain I won't be any kind of villain at all.'

So instead of hoping that Dr D. Void's schemes would work this time, Jewel and Toby always wanted them to fail. But Toby didn't think much of the Hero Squad either. When Jewel told him that Captain Excelsior was planning to go to Phoenix Park, he shrugged.

'The only reason those clowns always win is because your dad's plans are full of holes.'

'They're all idiots,' Jewel agreed. 'Prancing about in stupid outfits and giving themselves silly names. But it's stupid for Dad to try an evil scheme right in front of them. If they found out who was responsible he could get in a lot of trouble.'

But Toby wasn't listening. 'Using super-powers is like cheating,' he was saying. 'At least Doctor D. Void makes all his machines himself. Captain Excelsior is just lucky. You know, if I ran the city I'd have a law against anyone using superpowers at all.'

Jewel sighed. Toby was always talking about what he'd do if he ran the city, sometimes he went on for hours.

'Look,' she said. 'We're going to Phoenix Park on Saturday. Someone's got to keep an eye on Dad.'

That Saturday Ben couldn't believe it when his dad told him they were going to Phoenix Park.

'I've heard it's really something special,' Keith Carter said. 'So I thought we should go and take a look. That is, if you want to?'

'Of course I want to,' Ben said, grinning all over his face. 'Everyone in my class is going. They say it's going to be brilliant.'

31

'Then it's settled,' his dad said. 'Fay can drop us there on her way to work.'

Ben's grin faded a bit but he didn't say anything. Fay was his dad's girlfriend and he didn't like her very much. It wasn't because he wanted his parents to get back together, he knew that wasn't going to happen, but Fay was so stupid. She was a cheerleader for the Multiplicity Mammoths and had bambi-like brown eyes and fluffy red hair and a bouncy personality. She wore sparkly clothes and make-up that made her face look permanently surprised and she always spoke in exclamations.

She did it then, looking up from her healthy breakfast of fruit pieces in low-fat yoghurt.

'Gosh! Phoenix Park! That's so exciting! But I heard it might rain today! Perhaps you should go another time!'

Ben just stared at her. Through the windows of the apartment the sky showed a beautiful bright blue. He couldn't believe she was trying to spoil his day with such an idiotic remark. Sometimes he thought the only reason his dad was going out with Fay was because she was far too dim to realize that he looked exactly like Captain Excelsior.

'I don't think we need to worry about rain,' Keith said, with a smile. 'Besides, I don't know when I'll next get a free weekend. You will drop us off, won't you, Fay? It'll be impossible to park with everyone in Multiplicity going.'

'Of course I will!' Fay exclaimed. 'We can go straight after breakfast! Wow ... is that the time? I must go and get ready!'

Ben rolled his eyes but today he didn't care how silly Fay was being. He was going to Phoenix Park for a day out with his dad and outside the sun seemed to shine even brighter because of it.

His dad was right about parking being impossible. Fay took them to the turn-off for the park and even there the traffic was moving so slowly that they decided to get out and walk. Ben said 'thank you' and looked away while his dad kissed Fay goodbye. When her bright red Infernus 6000 had pulled away he grabbed his dad's arm and hurried him over to the ticket stalls. There was already a queue but it was moving quickly and before long they reached the front.

It was difficult to decide what ride to go on first. Phoenix Park was everything the adverts had promised it would be. Huge rollercoasters looped and twisted over their heads, there were stalls selling everything from ice-creams to toy laser guns, all around were signs painted in bright colours with pictures of lions or penguins or the names of rides. *Corkscrew Twizzer*, Ben read, looking at one group of signs, *Haunted Hall and the Ghost Walk, Astrodome and the Moon Shoot Chute.* He could hardly believe he was really here.

Then it happened. Somewhere in the distance there was a scream, followed by the sound of people shouting. Ben felt his heart sink as everyone around them turned to look and he bit his lip hard. Over on the other side of the park, the sunlight was gleaming extra brightly on something he thought at first was part of one of the rollercoasters.

It wasn't.

Stalking between the rides on eight razor-sharp legs, sunlight dazzling from the smooth surface of its body, was a gigantic metal spider. As Ben watched, it turned its round head and eight red laser beams shot out of its eyes

and hit the top of the Haunted Hall, setting it on fire.

Ben swallowed, but, before he could feel properly frightened, the enormous spider changed course and started heading away from them towards the rocket-shaped building of the Moon Shoot Chute. The people around them stopped shouting and stared instead but Ben's dad was already looking around anxiously.

'Dad?' Ben said, looking up at him, and Keith Carter frowned.

'Sorry, Ben,' he said. 'Look's as if our day out's not going to happen. Not until someone gets that thing sorted out.' Taking hold of Ben's arm he pushed him down on to a nearby bench. 'Stay here, OK. I'm just going to go and . . . see if I can find a park keeper or something. I'll be back in a minute.'

Then, before Ben could say anything, his dad had abandoned him and was running in the direction of the ticket office as fast as he could.

Ben felt tears start in his eyes and blinked furiously to stop them. Right now he didn't care one bit about the giant spider or the still-burning Haunted Hall or any of the people who might get hurt in the crowds. All he could think about was that his dad had done it again. Instead of a special day out he was left sitting here alone on a stupid bench while his dad went off to be a hero.

'Don't be frightened,' a woman from the crowd said in a reassuring voice, seeing Ben's expression. 'Captain Excelsior will save the day.'

'So what?' Ben said angrily, raising his head to glare at the speaker. 'He's not going to save my day, is he? My day's going to be completely ruined as usual!'

Ben sat on the bench and scuffed his trainers against the ground. The woman who had spoken to him had moved off in a huff when he'd been rude to her and everyone else was drifting away as well, either trying to find a safe place to watch the action or hiding from the spider as it kicked the Moon Shoot Chute over and jumped up and down on the bits. Ben watched people go and it was only after a few minutes that he realized that he wasn't completely alone.

Heading in the opposite direction from the crowds were two kids: a boy and a girl who looked like first year juniors. They were talking together furiously and neither of them noticed Ben as they walked towards him.

'One stupid strawberry ice-cream,' the girl was saying, tossing her short untidy hair. 'And I wanted chocolate anyway. Then she takes off. It's just not fair!'

'I didn't go on a single ride,' the boy complained almost at the same time, his breath coming wheezily when his voice rose. 'Just to look at the elephants, as if I couldn't look at elephants anytime I wanted back home. Then he only goes and rides off on one. What good's an elephant going to be against a giant spider, I ask you?'

Ben stared at the two kids, suddenly interested in what they were saying, and the little girl turned to glare at him.

'What are you goggling at?' she asked crossly.

Ben felt uncomfortable. 'Sorry,' he said. 'I didn't mean to stare. I just wondered . . . are your parents super heroes?'

Both of them glared at him now and the boy looked disgusted as well.

'You're not a reporter, are you?' he said. 'Because we're not allowed to talk to reporters are we, Pippa?'

'Even if we were, I wouldn't,' the girl answered. 'In fact, I was telling Marcus only yesterday the next person who asks me about my mother is going to get punched on the nose.'

She was at least two years younger than Ben but she had a skull and crossbones drawn in pen on her arm so he thought about his words carefully before trying again.

'Look, I don't mean to offend you,' he

explained. 'I just wondered because ... because my dad's a super hero too. He's Captain Excelsior.'

The two kids stared at him and after a moment the girl stopped glaring and looked thoughtful instead.

'Are you sure?' she asked. 'I didn't know he even had a son.'

'He might as well not have,' Ben said glumly, remembering how annoyed he was. 'He never admits that he's Captain Excelsior to me. It's always just some dumb excuse like he has to go and get a park warden.'

'Seriously?' The girl looked outraged, her face twisting into a grimace. 'That's awful. Our parents are always dumping us somewhere too but at least they say why.'

'Well, my dad rode away on a elephant, it would be hard to disguise that,' the boy said, sitting down next to Ben on the bench and taking out an inhaler. He had to take a couple of sharp breaths from it before he could speak again and while he was waiting the girl introduced herself.

'I'm Pippa Power,' she said. 'And this is Marcus Mondrian; his dad is Animo.'

As the screams and shouts continued from the other side of the park, she continued to talk and Ben listened in fascination.

Pippa Power was eight years old. She liked animals, horse-riding, and playing sports. She hated girly dresses, dolls, and the colour pink. Unfortunately, her mother was Princess Power.

As well as being second-in-command of the Hero Squad, Princess Power ran the Princess Power Toy Company. The toy company sold Princess Power dolls with waist length blonde hair, sparkly blue eyes, and matching pink accessories. They also made Princess Power posters, Princess Power jewellery, and Princess Power make-up. All over Multiplicity little girls slept under pink star duvets and dreamed of being just like Princess Power when they grew up.

Pippa's room was pink but she kept it in so much of a mess that it never looked good. Pippa's hair was mousy brown and she had cut it herself with nail-scissors so that it was ragged and untidy. Pippa had wardrobes full of pretty dresses with lace and frills but she always wore jeans and T-shirts and a pair of grubby trainers with broken laces. In fact, as Ben had already discovered, Pippa was about as unlike her mother as two people could be.

Or almost.

Marcus would have got on fine with Animo if he had been at all interested in animals or hiking or playing sport. The trouble was that Marcus was small, weedy, and wore great big glasses because his eyesight was so bad. He got hayfever when he went outside, being near animals gave him rashes or brought on his asthma, and he always fell over his own feet or dropped the ball when he played sports.

What Marcus enjoyed most was playing on his computer. But he didn't have any games with super heroes or wizards or warriors in them. He liked the kind of game where you had to build a civilization and teach your people how to make fire and build houses, and which you win by earning more points than anyone else.

'But Dad thinks computers are a waste of time,' he told Ben. 'He can't even use a DVD player. And he's never pleased when I get good marks at school. He only cares about sports and I'm useless at those.'

'He's not very good,' Pippa agreed. 'I beat him at football every time we play. But all my mum does is complain that my clothes are muddy or I didn't brush my hair.'

'And I'm useless at everything,' Ben said miserably. 'That's why my dad's ashamed of me. He's a hero and I'm a zero.'

Pippa and Marcus looked at him sympathetically and then at each other. Neither of them could think of anything to say. They'd both been annoyed at not getting the chance to enjoy the park but, in comparison to Ben, their problems didn't seem so bad. Could it really be true that Captain Excelsior was ashamed of his son?

Meanwhile, Jewel and Toby were watching the gigantic spider with the rest of the crowds from a safe spot beneath the Corkscrew Twizzler. It was creating a trail of devastation, using the razor edges of its legs to cut things down and shooting red beams from its eyes to set things on fire.

'What's the point of it?' Toby asked indignantly, shaking his head. 'How's attacking

Phoenix Park supposed to help Doctor D. Void conquer the city?'

'I think it's supposed to be a nuisance,' Jewel said thoughtfully. 'That if it causes enough damage, the mayor will pay him to stop it, or something like that.'

'Well, it's idiotic,' Toby said sharply. 'I could come up with a better evil plan than that standing on my head. In fact, I can think of about ten things better than that right now . . .'

'Well, don't tell them to me,' Jewel said sharply. 'I have to listen to enough of that from my father. At least it doesn't look as if anyone's hurt, even though those silly idiots are just standing around watching it. What are they waiting for anyway?'

'For the Hero Squad,' Toby pointed out. 'Everyone expects them to turn up and stop it. It's all just a show to them. They don't take evil schemes seriously.'

He was right. Some of the people in the crowd had started to laugh. The spider had put a leg through the skylight of the astrodome and was now going in circles. It flailed its other legs wildly, just like a real spider, trying to get free.

'Sad, isn't it?' said Jewel, feeling embarrassed for her father.

'It's very realistic, at least,' Toby said sympathetically. 'Anyway, that antigravity device he had last week was pretty clever, the way he used it to float all the gold out of the bank vault.'

'Right up until it collapsed under the weight,' Jewel replied.

Just then a shout went up from the waiting crowds and Jewel and Toby turned to see three figures arrive, approaching the giant spider. Captain Excelsior's distinctive silhouette was outlined against the sun as he flew down out of the sky; Animo came out of the zoo enclosure riding an elephant, which trumpeted loudly in response to the crowd; Princess Power swooped through the air in a balletic pose, her jetpack spilling a trail of pink smoke behind her. Everyone could hear Captain Excelsior as he shouted:

'Something with as many legs as you should know when it's time to run away.'

The spider didn't even seem to have noticed. It had freed its trapped leg and was crouched in the astrodome plaza while the super heroes above it seemed to be organizing something that looked a bit like a massive parachute.

'I think it's a net,' Toby said, shading his eyes against the sun as he watched. 'I'm surprised it's not an enormous cup and a massive piece of paper, to be honest.'

They watched as the super heroes got the net unfolded and cast it over the spider. The spider tried to stand up underneath it and got its legs tangled instead and Animo's elephant started to haul it away. The spider's legs waggled unhappily from the net one final time before going still.

The crowds cheered wildly and Jewel and Toby backed out of the crush of people. Just as they had predicted, the Hero Squad had defeated yet another of Dr D. Void's evil schemes.

'What a waste of time,' Toby said as they headed for the exit. 'Your father might as well not have bothered.'

'It was completely dim-witted to set off the spider in Phoenix Park,' Jewel agreed. 'Especially when the Fade *told* him Captain Excelsior would be here. Besides, it's just spoiled a lot of people's day out.'

'Come on, they think it's exciting,' Toby objected, looking back at the crowds, but Jewel touched his arm and pointed at a group of figures sitting on a bench near the ticket stands.

'Those three don't look very happy,' she said.

Ben looked up with a scowl as two people detached themselves from the crowd and

headed over to him. Marcus patted his arm in a consoling way and Pippa stood up in front of him defensively.

'Um, I'm Jewel and this is my friend Toby,' the girl said, looking strangely embarrassed. She had long shiny black hair and she fiddled with a strand of it awkwardly. 'I hope the spider thing didn't spoil your day . . .'

'What do you know about it?' Ben asked angrily, glaring at her. 'It did spoil my day and probably my entire life. So there.'

'Well, it's all over,' Toby said with a shrug. 'The Hero Squad caught it, so that's that.'

'It's over for *now*,' Pippa said crossly. 'But something else just as bad will probably happen tomorrow.'

'She's right,' Marcus agreed. 'There's always something. Honestly, I wish just one week could go by with nothing super or villainous happening at *all*.'

Ben sighed, slouching down on the bench, and Jewel looked upset, twisting her loose strand of hair round and round in her hand.

'I really am sorry,' she said. 'I feel responsible . . .'

'I don't know why,' Ben said, frowning at her.

'Yeah,' Pippa agreed. 'It's super heroes who cause all the trouble, flying around like idiots and filling up the place with pink smoke.'

'Prancing about in costumes and riding around on elephants,' Marcus added.

'Leaving people to sit on stupid benches while they go and save the city for the ten billionth time,' Ben finished angrily.

Jewel and Toby looked at the others, finally realizing who they were talking to. Only super heroes' children could possibly sound so bitter about them.

'You hate super heroes?' Jewel said after a moment. 'Well, arch villains are just as bad, believe me. All they care about is taking over the city and they won't listen, no matter how many times you tell them it's not going to work.'

'And henchmen,' Toby added. 'Henchmen and henchwomen, all they ever tell you is "do what the boss says, do what the boss says" even when the boss is saying something completely stupid.'

'I am really sorry about the spider,' Jewel said, looking at Ben. 'But my father just can't help inventing evil plans. He enjoys it.'

'And my father never tells him that they're not going to work,' Toby added. 'Even when it's obvious.'

Ben looked at Jewel and Toby and then at Marcus and Pippa. They were all miserable and so was he. But suddenly he was tired of feeling unhappy all the time. Up until now he'd thought he was the only person in Multiplicity who didn't enjoy the excitement of the Hero Squad defeating villainous schemes. But now he'd met four other people who felt the same way.

'We should do something about it,' he said out loud. 'About super heroes and arch villains too. We should do something to stop them messing us about.'

'But isn't it villains who try to stop heroes?' Toby asked doubtfully. 'And heroes who try to stop villains? There's not room for anyone else in between.'

'I don't see why not.' Jewel was looking enthusiastic and she smiled at Ben, making him blush a bit. 'There's all the normal people, right? Someone should stand up for them. All of this hero-villain business is wrecking the city.'

'We could form a new team,' Pippa said, nodding fiercely. 'Against both sides. Our mission could be to embarrass all our parents!'

'Or at least stop them embarrassing us all the time,' Marcus agreed, looking suddenly cheerful. 'I'd join something like that, definitely.'

They all turned towards Ben and their faces were serious. Looking from Jewel's green eyes to Toby's muscled arms, Pippa's skull and crossbones, and Marcus's expression gleaming with mischief, Ben thought they made a pretty cool team.

'So everyone's in, right?' Pippa asked and the others nodded.

'We can all come up with plans to stop the heroes *and* the villains,' Marcus added. 'And give the rest of us a break.'

'But we should have a name,' Toby said. 'To say what we stand for.'

'What do you think?' Jewel asked, looking at Ben. 'It was your idea so you should be the leader.'

Ben realized that was true. Suddenly he'd made friends and instead of being picked last he was actually in charge of something.

'I know what we should be called,' he said. 'We should be the Zeroes. Because without zero nothing else counts.' He put out his hand and the others put theirs on top of his. 'There's nothing wrong with being normal,' he said, grinning for the first time since his dad had left him on the bench. 'And the Zeroes are going to make everyone believe it.'

3
To the Power of Five

It took the Super Zeroes a little while to arrange their first meeting. For a start, they couldn't let any of their parents find out what was going on. In the end it was Jewel who thought of a way to make sure they would be able to talk in private.

'Why don't we meet the next time my father is carrying out one of his plans,' she told Toby. 'He'll be busy in the lair and all the Hero Squad will be out trying to thwart him.'

'He's always got some kind of plan,' Toby agreed. 'The next one is putting green stuff in the water system to make it bubble out and cover the city in goo.'

'That sounds useful,' Jewel said, rolling her eyes. 'When is the green goo supposed to come bubbling out?'

'Next Saturday,' said Toby. 'At exactly midday. My dad's in charge of Bubble Machine Four. He's annoyed about it because none of the henchmen are getting overtime.'

'Good, then we'll leave early in the morning,' Jewel said. 'So we won't get caught in the goo.'

Jewel phoned Ben to tell him about the goo plan and ask where they should meet up. She had the same kind of video phone that Ben's dad had given him and she pressed extra buttons so she could call the others at the same time. On his regular phone Ben couldn't see their faces but he could hear their voices, as they all agreed Jewel's idea was a good one.

'Can't we meet at the lair?' Marcus asked. 'I bet it's full of cool machines and things.'

'But I want to go to your house and feed the animals,' Pippa protested.

'We have to make it somewhere where we won't be noticed,' Ben said, 'by heroes or villains or anyone who works for them.'

'My house is big,' said Marcus. 'But it's full of zookeepers and lion tamers and snake charmers and people like that.'

'I suppose it'll have to be mine then,' Pippa said miserably. 'There's just me and a bunch of pink robots.'

Ben had been going to say they could meet at his house. It would have been cool for his mother to see that he had friends. But suddenly he thought he'd actually like to see a proper super hero's house, so he agreed they should meet at Pippa's.

'I'll tell the robots I'm having some friends round,' Pippa said. 'So there'll be some food at least, although I can't promise it'll be very nice.'

Early on Saturday morning Jewel and Toby sneaked out of the lair by one of the secret entrances. They chose one that connected to the underground train system and took a train to the expensive part of town, where Power Towers was. The train ride took a long time, which was unusual. Instead of zipping through the tunnels with a zooming sound, the train chugged and grinded and made awful screeching noises whenever it stopped at a station. All the passengers were cross and confused. But once when the train stopped for a long time in a tunnel, Toby peered out of the window into the darkness. When he sat back down his face was glum.

'I saw stuff glowing in the tunnel,' he whispered to Jewel. 'Green stuff. I think the goo might have escaped.'

Ben had come by bus. That had taken a long time as well. The robotic buses of Multiplicity were very clean and efficient; they whirred and buzzed from bus stop to bus stop collecting people. Today the bus kept missing stops and then sitting down in the middle of the road for a long time while passing cars honked and swerved around it. The conductor had to keep getting down and poking about in the machinery under the bus to make it move again. When they finally got to his stop, Ben got down quickly and turned to look at the machinery too.

It was all gummed up with greenish coloured goo.

Marcus had come by giant eagle. It hadn't been his idea. Animo thought it wasn't safe for him to walk around on the streets that day, or go by bus or train or car.

'I've heard that some strange things are happening in the city, son,' he said. 'Captain Excelsior suspects it may be another villainous plan.'

Although Marcus tried to argue, Animo was having none of it. He harnessed the giant eagle with a special sort of swing seat and made Marcus sit in it.

'I'm sending you to Power Towers,' he said. 'You'll be safe there . . . Hold on tight!' he shouted as the eagle took off, flapping its enormous wings to gain height.

Marcus saw the whole city spinning and swinging beneath his dangling feet. Here and there were patches of green of a particularly noxious vomit colour. Clinging as tightly as he could to the straps of the swing he closed his eyes and hoped he'd get to Power Towers soon.

Power Towers was surrounded by high walls and the main entrance was a tall gate with an intercom system. Behind the gate you could see towers and battlements and balconies, all crammed in on every side of the palace so that no part of it was undecorated. It was very pink. The walls, the towers, the gate, the balconies: all pink. It shone in the morning sunshine like a gigantic salmon mousse.

Ben met Jewel and Toby at the main gate just as they were pressing a button on the pink intercom. Pippa's voice came out of it saying crossly, 'Who's there?'

'It's us,' Ben said. 'Me and Jewel and Toby.'

'I'll open the gate,' Pippa's voice replied. 'Marcus is already here. He's being sick.'

The intercom clicked off and the gate slid smoothly open. Exchanging looks, the three of them walked up the drive of pink gravel, past the pink flowerbeds, and up to the pink door. It opened as they reached it and they saw a robot standing in the rose-marble hall.

Jewel and Toby were used to robots. Dr D. Void used them all the time in his plots. But this was a kind of robot they'd never seen before. It was six feet tall and covered from head to foot in pink fur. Its eyes were shiny gold and its mouth stretched in a wide grin.

'Eeep,' Jewel said, taking a step back and nearly falling over when she ran into Ben. 'What *is* that?'

'It's really scary,' Toby said admiringly. 'Is it evil, do you think?'

'My name is Poppet,' the robot said in a sing-song voice. 'I'm so happy to meet you. Please come this way.'

It turned round and started to walk up the curving flight of rose-marble stairs.

'I think it's supposed to be sweet,' Ben said, helping Jewel stand up again.

'I don't like it,' Jewel said, eyeing the robot uncertainly. 'It's creepy.'

'It's awesome,' Toby said admiringly. 'Much better than Doctor D. Void's robots.'

Poppet led them up three floors to one of the tower rooms. All the carpets were pink, the banisters and door handles were gold, and the walls of the palace had massive mirrors from floor to ceiling. Jewel kept jumping whenever she saw an unexpected reflection of the pink robot behind her. Finally they reached Pippa's room and the robot stopped.

'Have a happy happy fun time,' it chirped as it opened the door for them. 'Please call if you need anything.'

Inside the room Pippa was waiting for them with a scowl on her face in the middle of piles and piles of stuff. Dirty clothes and footballs and crisp packets and all sorts of junk lay strewn about the room. They almost covered the pretty four-poster bed and the pink computer on a gold dressing table and the wardrobe painted with fairies in pink dresses with golden hair. Through an open door on the other side of the room they could see a gleaming pink bathroom from which came the sound of someone being violently sick.

After all the pink, Ben was feeling a bit sick himself.

'Hi, Pippa, is Marcus OK?' he asked, sympathetically.

'His stupid dad sent him here on a giant eagle,' Pippa explained. 'Marcus can't stand heights.'

Just then Marcus came into the room. His face was slightly green and his eyes were big and scared.

'Everything was spinning,' he said weakly. 'Around and around and around.'

'You'd better sit down,' Jewel told him and helped him to a squashy pink sofa, covered with a pile of black T-shirts.

She sat down next to him and said, 'I'm not feeling too good myself after seeing that robot thing.'

61

'Poppet?' Pippa said. 'Yeah, well, I warned you. The palace is full of fluffy pink robots. They make all the Princess Power toys.' She went over to a tray of food and asked, 'Does anyone want anything to eat? We've got doughnuts or cake or ice-cream, all sorts. But I'm afraid it's all pink.'

Sitting back in a comfortable chair eating a pink-iced doughnut with a strawberry milkshake next to him, Ben had to admit that there were some good things about Power Towers. Marcus had recovered from his fright and was showing Toby all the cool electronic stuff in the room: not just the food dispenser and the computer but things like rocket-boots and power-skates that Pippa had buried in the back of her wardrobe.

'I like it much more here than the zoo,' he said, taking a deep breath. 'It would be an excellent place to live if it wasn't for the pink.'

'In a weird way it reminds me of Dad's lair,' Jewel agreed. 'That's all black furniture and white cats . . . I never thought I'd say it but even that's better than this.'

'That's probably because Power Towers isn't just a house,' Pippa said. 'It's a factory as well. Poppet and the other robots make the toys for the Princess Power toy company here and all the gizmos and gadgets Mum uses in her hero work. There's tonnes of rocket launchers and ray guns and smoke grenades and all sorts in the basement, not to mention all the dolls.'

'This is cool though,' Toby said. He'd opened up the back of a Princess Power doll and was looking at the electronic circuitry inside. 'The computer chips in this are Spirit Sixes, the best you can get.'

'It's ghastly,' Pippa said flatly. 'Listen to this.' Reaching out she pressed a button on the doll's tummy and bouncy jingly music started to play and the doll sang:

'The Hero Squad are strong and brave.
If you're in trouble we will save
You, because we care
About everybody everywhere.'

Toby quickly switched the doll off again and dropped it on the floor. They all looked at it with disgust.

'All right,' Ben said. 'Pippa's right. It's awful.' He shook his head. 'Caring about everybody? Everybody except us, more like.'

'So what are we going to do about it?' Pippa demanded. She hadn't eaten anything until Jewel had brought out a box of dark chocolates from her backpack and shared them around. 'I'm going mad here. I think if I have to eat another cherry jelly or speak to another soppy robot I'll scream.'

'I'm not getting back on that eagle,' Marcus added. 'It makes me feel ill just thinking about it.'

'And it's embarrassing watching every single one of Dad's plans mess up,' Jewel agreed. 'Did you see the green goo on the way here? I just know it's going to go horribly wrong somehow.'

'Well, that's what we're here for, isn't it?' asked Toby. 'To find a way to stop our parents from messing up our lives all the time.'

Everyone turned to look at Ben and he gulped. He was supposed to be in charge of the group and so far he hadn't had even one idea.

Thinking fast, he said out loud, 'That's right. So, what ideas has everyone had about how to get our parents to stop showing off their powers all the time?'

To his surprise everyone started talking at once. It sounded as if they'd all been thinking about it much harder than he had and as he listened to the suggestions Ben tried hard to think of one of his own.

'I was wondering about opening all the cages in Dad's zoo,' Marcus said. 'And setting all the animals free. Without them, he wouldn't be Animo any more.'

'I'd like to get into the toy factory and paint all the Princess Power dolls black,' Pippa added. 'And make them sing something about how the Hero Squad suck.'

'If I could find a way to thwart all my father's evil plans while they were still in the lab, then maybe he'd give up on them,' Jewel said.

'Or make him think that other people were even better at evil plans than he was,' Toby said thoughtfully.

Ben had been listening carefully. It sounded as if everyone had their own scheme already. In fact, Toby was still talking about ideas he'd had for lots and lots of plans. But being part of a team meant working together.

'Those are really good ideas,' he said. 'But wouldn't it be even better if we could add all the plans up together?' he suggested.

'That's a good idea if we can manage it,' Jewel said admiringly and Ben blushed.

'Let's get a big piece of paper and write down everything we can think of,' Toby said. 'Then we can draw lines between the parts that might work together.'

Pippa got out a really big piece of pink paper and Marcus found some pens and pencils and they all started writing the things down. Ben watched the others scribbling away enviously. Toby had already written down ten different ideas by the time Ben took a pen. Jewel was drawing a line between her own *'Get rid of pathetic evil robots'* and Pippa's *'Get rid of pink fluffy robots'*. Finally Ben wrote down the only idea he had:

'Make Captain Excelsior reveal his true identity . . .'

By the end of the afternoon they had come up with a final plan. It was Toby who'd thought of the ways to link up all the different parts, but Pippa and Marcus had both been really inventive and Jewel had said they could use all sorts of things from Dr D. Void's lair to make it work. But it was Ben's idea that made all the parts suddenly make sense.

'That's really evil,' Pippa said grinning.

'That's really brave,' Jewel said at the same time.

'Let's just hope it works,' Ben told them and everyone crossed their fingers.

On the way home Ben saw that the streets were clean. On the bus, all the passengers were talking about how Captain Excelsior had burnt all the goo out of the mechanism with his laser vision.

Marcus walked home with the eagle following, shrieking at him all the way. The green patches of goo he'd seen from the air were melting underneath pink fluffy foam like candyfloss. By the time he got to his house he was feeling sick again.

On the train home Jewel and Toby had heard an announcement that Animo had brought a tribe of monkeys into the tunnels to clear up the goo.

'Poor monkeys,' Jewel said as they reached the entrance to Dr D. Void's secret lair.

'Poor us,' said Toby as the automatic doors opened and they saw what was inside.

The secret lair was covered with green goo, two feet deep. The black leather chairs were slimy and smelt horrible. White angora cats were hissing and spitting from the top of furniture, their fur gummed up with green slime. As they waded through the goo Jewel bumped into someone invisible.

'Is that you, Fade?' she asked. 'What's going on?'

'Doctor D. Void forgot that the secret base isn't properly sealed,' the invisible agent replied. 'And he ordered all the henchmen to speed up the bubble generators when he heard the heroes were getting rid of the goo and quite a lot of it leaked in.'

'What did the doctor say?' Toby asked.

'You can probably guess,' the Fade sighed.

Jewel nodded.

'I'll get you next time, Hero Squad,' she said, sadly.

4
Undivided Attention

The Super Zeroes' plan began the next day. On Sunday night Jewel and Toby logged on to the secret lair computer system. Toby had guessed Dr D. Void's password on his second try.

'That's not very imaginative,' he said as he typed in the letters E V I L. 'Almost anything would have been better than that.'

'Do you think the plan will really work?' Jewel had asked. 'I mean, Dad really likes being evil. What if we end up making him even more competitive about it?'

'Relax,' Toby said. 'I'm not so sure he does like being evil. I think it's mostly just inventing stuff that he enjoys. You know he never uses the same plan twice. If one goes wrong he never uses it again, even if it was just one tiny thing that didn't work.'

As he spoke he was scrolling down the list of computer files. There were hundreds of them. Plans for making every kind of mutant; designs for every kind of car, tank, train, plane, or giant digging machine, and a saved copy of every computer virus Dr D. Void had ever used.

'That's the one we want,' Jewel said, pointing at the screen as the text scrolled past. 'Robot Rampage.'

'Great work,' Toby said, selecting the file and attaching it to the email program.

To: pippa@powertowers.zap he typed. **Here's the file you need. Good luck!**

Jewel crossed her fingers and Toby did too. Then he took a deep breath and pressed the button to send the email.

'That's the beginning,' Jewel said, as she and Toby crept back to their rooms. 'It's up to Pippa and Marcus now.'

Marcus had arranged to spend the night at Pippa's house and he was working on Pippa's computer when the email arrived.

'It's here!' he said. 'Jewel and Toby did it!'

'Hurry up and get it on the disks,' Pippa said, leaning over his shoulder. 'I can't wait to see it in action.'

Toby carefully loaded two CDs into the computer and copied the program on to them. They had to wait a while for the computer to finish whirring and clunking but finally it ejected the disks and Pippa put each one in a clear pink case. Then they crept quietly out of Pippa's room and down to the basement.

Even though it was the middle of the night, Poppet and the other robots were hard at work. As Pippa and Marcus sneaked past the armoury they could see huge fluffy robots refilling Degoopenators with pink foam; others were recharging the pink rocket packs the princess used, still more were adjusting laser pistols to a shade just between puce and fuchsia. When the children reached the basement they found even more robots packing up hundreds of Princess Power dolls to be sent out to toy shops the next day. Poppet was in charge and Pippa could hear its high squeaky voice saying, 'Isn't this an exciting job? Think of all the lucky boys and girls who'll be able to enjoy these lovely toys.'

'And thanks to us they'll enjoy them even more,' Pippa whispered to Marcus before going into the room in a rush and faking a worried expression.

'Oh, Poppet,' Pippa said. 'I'm glad I found you. Mum forgot to give you this computer disk and she said it's very important this program is installed on all the new dolls. It's a brand new song about caring and sharing.'

'Goody gumdrops!' squeaked the robot as it took the disk. 'Oooh, I can't wait to hear it!'

Pippa and Toby rolled their eyes at each other behind its back.

'And I have a special present for you and

the other robots, Poppet,' Marcus added. 'The princess said this other disk is a reward for all your hard work. There's a program on it that's just like a . . . a lovely hug.' He wasn't as good an actor as Pippa but it didn't seem to matter.

'Isn't that just super nice of the princess?' Poppet squeaked. 'We'll run the program as soon as we've finished with the dolls . . .'

The next morning Ben rushed downstairs and turned on the television as soon as he was up and dressed.

'You'll be late for school,' his mother warned him, as she got ready to go to work. 'Turn that off and come and have breakfast.'

'I have to watch the news, Mum,' Ben insisted. 'It's for a . . . a school project.'

His mother opened her mouth, probably to say he hadn't told her anything about this mysterious project before, but then the news came on and her mouth just stayed open.

The reporter was standing in front of a toy

shop with lots of tiny holes in the outside wall. It looked more like a Swiss cheese than a shop.

'In breaking news this morning,' he was saying. *'We've received reports that toy shops and shopping malls all over the city have been damaged just like this one. Mysteriously, the only missing stock is the entire shipment of Princess Power dolls. It is estimated that the damage will cost thousands of pounds to repair.'*

'YES!' Ben said, punching the air, and his mum gave him a cross look.

'Those dolls are pretty awful,' she said. 'But a lot of property was damaged and what if people had been hurt. It's really not funny, Ben.'

Ben made his face serious and sad but just then Captain Excelsior came on the news and he didn't have to pretend any more.

'I won't rest until we've brought to justice those responsible for this crime,' he said. *'The children of this city love those toys.'* Ben made a face at the screen.

'Come on, darling,' his mum said, ruffling his hair as she turned the TV off. 'Time to get ready for school.'

Ben went and had his breakfast and got his

packed lunch ready but as he left the house he was grinning again.

'You look happy,' his mum said. 'Is something good happening today?'

'That's right,' he said. 'Today we're going to prove the most important number is zero.'

When Captain Excelsior had finished giving interviews to all the reporters he flew to Hero Heights, where the Hero Squad had their base. The main control room was full of dogs. There were Alsatians and Dalmatians, bloodhounds and wolfhounds, lurchers, pointers, and terriers, all running around sniffing each other and the computer equipment. Captain Excelsior had to push his way through them as he came into the room.

Animo was on the phone to the mayor.

'. . . yes, Mr Mayor,' he was saying. 'Don't worry. The Hero Squad will get to the bottom of this.'

As Animo put down the phone, Captain Excelsior frowned thoughtfully, patting one of the dogs.

'Somehow this doesn't seem the usual style of

evil plot,' he said. 'What kind of villain steals children's toys?'

Animo shrugged and flexed his muscles.

'One who hates children?' he suggested. 'But why is it only the Princess Power dolls that have gone missing?'

'Perhaps the princess has an idea.' Captain Excelsior looked around. 'Where is she, anyway?'

'No idea,' Animo said. 'I thought she'd be here by now. I tried phoning her but one of those weird fluffy robots picked up and I couldn't get any sense out of it.'

'Hmm,' Captain Excelsior said, stroking his chin. 'I think I'd better go to Power Towers and find the princess. It's not like her not to show up when there's trouble at hand.'

'Good plan,' Animo agreed. 'I'll go and check out the toy shops. These are all trained sniffer dogs.' He looked proudly at the pack of dogs filling the room. 'Whoever the villain is, they'll have left some kind of trail which the dogs can follow.'

'The princess and I will come and find you there,' Captain Excelsior agreed.

Privately he was relieved that the dogs were

there for a reason. As well as all the animals in the Menagerie, Animo was constantly filling the Hero Heights swimming pool with sharks or the garage with wildebeest and Captain Excelsior hadn't been at all happy to find a tarantula nest in his sock drawer once.

As the captain flew away, Animo told the dogs to follow him and he set off for the nearest toy shop. Inside, the staff were clearing rubbish and Animo realized it was all pink. Bending down he picked up a piece of packaging. It was from the Princess Power dolls. On the pink cardboard words were printed in gold letters.

YOUR VERY OWN PRINCESS POWER DOLL TO
    TREASURE . . .
LONG-LIFE BATTERIES INCLUDED . . .
ROCKET PACK MAKES REAL PINK SMOKE ! . . .
DOLL WALKS AND TALKS . . .
BOW AND 12 GOLD ARROWS INCLUDED . . .
PRINCESS SINGS 10 DIFFERENT SONGS . . .
NOW WITH NEW 'LET'S ALL GO TO THE ZOO'
    SONG . . .

Animo shrugged and dropped it. He wondered why whoever had stolen the dolls had taken them out of the packaging first.

'Any signs of breaking and entering?' he asked the manager and the man glared at him.

'Just those!' she said, pointing at the hundreds of holes broken in the bottom of the walls. 'What can have taken them? It's as if they were stolen by mice.'

'The mice of this city have no interest in children's toys,' Animo said firmly. 'Besides, mice couldn't break through walls.' He took a closer look at the holes and peeled loose a tiny piece of golden hair caught in the rubble. It wasn't real hair though, just gold cotton.

Calling to the dogs he gathered them outside the building and pointed them at one of the holes.

'*What do you smell?*' he asked the dogs telepathically, and they cast about for a scent.

'*Plastic! Smoke! Cotton! Brick dust!*'

'*Nothing else?*' Animo insisted. '*Only the doll smells?*'

'*It leads this way!*' the dogs replied, eager to be off and running, and Animo shrugged.

'*All right, follow the trail,*' he decided and set off at a run as the dogs leapt away.

The trail led straight towards the Multiplicity Zoo and as they got closer Animo began to hear a loud noise. It took him a moment to realize he could hear it in his mind as well as his ears. It was the sound of hundreds of animals panicking. Something had happened which had frightened them, and it was still going on.

Animo ran faster, and as he followed the dogs around a corner they yelped in surprise. A group of hippos was charging up the street, knocking people out of the way. Animo tried to send a burst of calming thought their way but there's almost nothing as dangerous as an angry hippo and it was hard to be calm. He and the dogs were tossed aside as the hippos barged past and up the street.

Animo got up in time to see an elephant galloping towards him and jumped out of the way. The dogs had scattered, as panicked as the people, and Animo hurried on to the zoo. The walls were damaged in the same way the toy shop had been, and there were even larger holes too, made by charging animals. The noise inside was incredible. Every single animal enclosure had been broken open and the animals were everywhere; flocks and herds and prides and packs were surging around and about, screeching, mooing, roaring, and barking.

'Thank goodness!' a zookeeper shouted as he recognized Animo. 'You have to do something! It's as if they've all gone crazy.'

'The animals are frightened,' Animo explained. 'I'm trying to send calming thoughts but they're too panicked to hear me. What did this?'

'It was dolls,' the zookeeper gasped. 'I saw them. Hundreds of tiny pink and gold dolls, all singing a song about going to the zoo.'

'The missing Princess Power dolls? They did this?'

Animo tried to think but the noise of so many animals made it impossible.

'I can't stay,' he explained. 'I have to find out what the robots are doing . . . I'll try and think of something to help these animals but you'll have to do your best until then.'

'Hey!' the zookeeper shouted after him as Animo left. 'You're Animo, aren't you? What's so heroic about running away!'

Animo ignored him: he was having a horrible thought. If the dolls were destroying animal enclosures there was one obvious place for them to go next . . .

Meanwhile Captain Excelsior was flying to Power Towers. As it shimmered in the morning sunlight he noticed it was looking even pinker than usual but it was not until he reached the gates that he saw what was different. The front courtyard of the palace was full of robots. Eight-foot tall pink fluffy robots holding pink weapons. Captain Excelsior recognized those robots, they were the ones that worked in the factory part of the building. Then he realized he recognized some of those weapons as well. There were ray guns and rocket launchers, giant net shooters and flame-throwers, all with Princess Power's 'PP' symbol marked in gold.

Circling the building, he looked down at the robots, feeling worried. He'd always found them a little alarming and now they were obviously armed and dangerous; some of them had already spotted him and were taking pot shots at him. He wondered how many of them there were; the whole place seemed to be covered in pink fluff, as if Power Towers had grown fur.

Dodging a jet of flame, Captain Excelsior called down to one of the robots.

'What do you robots think you're doing?'

'We're rampaging,' the pink robot claimed in a surprisingly squeaky voice. 'Then we're going to help the princess take over the world! And we'll all have a really happy fun time doing it.'

Captain Excelsior couldn't believe it. Princess Power wanting to take over the world? It was impossible. But as several robots opened fire with their ray guns, it was clear that they believed it. In fact robots were already streaming out of the gates, obviously preparing the first stage of their world domination plan. Ducking and diving through the rays, the captain used his own laser vision to fire back at the robots and weld the gates of Power Towers shut. It wouldn't hold them for long, though, not with the weapons they had.

Suddenly something pink came up from one side, and he sent a streaking *zap* of laser beams at it.

'Don't shoot! It's me!' a familiar voice called as the pink thing swerved to avoid the lasers. Captain Excelsior realized it was Princess Power, wearing her pink costume and jetpack.

'Princess!' he said, flying towards her. 'I hope I didn't hurt you. I'm so sorry . . . with all these robots going crazy down there it's not the best time to be wearing pink.'

'I thought for a moment you didn't trust me,' Princess Power said, looking unhappy. 'Poppet and the robots from my toy factory seem to have gone insane. They seem to think I want to rule the world!'

'They told me that too,' Captain Excelsior admitted. 'But I didn't believe it for a moment. I came here because I was worried about you.'

'Oh, the robots haven't hurt me,' Princess Power told him. 'But they won't obey my orders any more and they've taken all my weapons. I've no idea how to stop them taking over the city.'

Captain Excelsior shook his head in confusion.

'Something very strange is going on,' he said. 'We'd better get back to Hero Heights as fast as we can.'

Deep down in his secret lair Doctor D. Void had been working on his latest invention: a giant catapult that would shoot Captain Excelsior out into space. Terry Tench, his henchman, was passing the doctor tools and very carefully not asking how he planned to get Captain Excelsior on board the catapult in the first place. They had just taken their mid-morning coffee break and Dr D. Void was fishing a ball of cat fur out of his cup when there was a newsflash on one of his television screens.

'*Attention all citizens,*' it said. '*A horde of robots is rampaging across the city.*'

Dr D. Void frowned.

'We don't have any robots scheduled for today, do we?' he asked.

'No, Doctor. Ours were all crushed by rhinoceroses last month,' Terry told him. 'We're still waiting for the new ones to be delivered.'

'*Citizens are advised to stay in their homes or workplaces,*' the newsreader continued. '*The robots are over six feet tall, pink, fluffy and highly aggressive. Under no circumstances should they be approached. If you see one please contact this emergency number.*'

The emergency number came up on the screen underneath an image of pink robots swarming over the football stadium, pulling it to pieces and shrieking in squeaky voices. Dr D. Void raised his eyebrows.

'Pink?' he said. 'What kind of respectable robot is pink?'

'They seem to be working though,' Terry said unwisely, as the football stadium collapsed in a cloud of dust.

D. Void ground his teeth.

'I'm supposed to be the one who destroys this city,' he said. 'How dare another villain build evil robots without checking with me first.'

'Boss, look at that!' Terry said, pointing at a different TV screen. This one was showing the city zoo, filled with rioting animals. Dr D. Void turned the sound up in time to hear a different news reporter saying:

'. . . scenes of chaos at the city zoo. Keepers are struggling to contain the animals and many have escaped on to the streets. Meanwhile the super hero, Animo, was unavailable for comment and reports just coming in are saying that there are similar scenes of devastation at his own Menagerie. Witness reports claim that the damage was caused by an invasion of tiny dolls, dressed in pink, with long golden hair . . .'

Dr D. Void shifted a cat off the remote control and turned all the other channels to news.

'Pink again,' he muttered. 'Pink, pink, pink . . .'

Just then one of the screens focused on Power Towers, apparently covered with a giant fur blanket. D. Void stared at all the robots waving weapons as the announcer said:

'News just in from Power Towers: the robot army's leader, Poppet, has announced they are helping Princess Power achieve world domination. Could the Hero Squad have turned evil? Our reporters will bring you the news as it breaks . . .'

'EVIL?' D. Void yelled. 'I'm EVIL. How dare those do-gooders change sides?'

He slammed his fist on his computer console and there was a yowl as the cat who'd been sitting there turned and sank its teeth into his hand.

After the emergency newsflash all the children at Pippa and Marcus's school were sent home for the day. The kids, who normally clustered around the Hero Squad's children asking for autographs, gave them some very strange looks on the school bus during the ride home. But they didn't care.

'We've done it!' Pippa whispered excitedly. 'We've really done it. After this no one will want to see a pink robot or buy a stupid Princess Power doll. They'll be too scared!'

'And my dad won't be able to be Animo any more,' Marcus whispered back. 'Not if everyone thinks his powers are useless. Perhaps he'll get a normal job like a banker or a builder.'

'I'd better come to your house,' Pippa added. 'Poppet will be even more insane than normal since we gave it Dr D. Void's world domination program.'

Animo's zoo was strangely quiet when they arrived. Normally they walked up to the mansion past compounds full of animals. Zebras and horses would neigh and come up in hope of a carrot; birds and monkeys would chirrup or chatter at them; and lions and tigers would be basking in the warm sunshine. Today there was nothing but broken enclosures and echoing silence.

Pippa felt a bit sad. Animo's zoo was her favourite place to escape from all the pink at the palace.

'I suppose the dolls frightened all the animals away,' she said. 'I can guess how they felt. Sometimes I have nightmares that I'm being chased by hundreds of tiny Princess Power dolls.'

But Marcus took a deep breath of air and smiled.

'No more asthma attacks,' he said grinning. 'No more eagles taking me to your house. No more stinky animal poo.'

At the house Marcus's mum came to open the door. Melissa Mondrian was a beautiful woman with coffee-coloured skin and dark brown hair, which she usually wore in complicated twisted braids. But today her hair was scrunched back in an untidy ponytail and her face was anxious and tired.

'Oh, Marcus, I'm glad you brought Pippa back with you,' she said. 'I've been so worried about your father, I forgot to call the school and ask them to send her here.'

'Where is Dad?'

'He's gone to Hero Heights but I don't know what he can do to help. The city's so full of frightened animals that it's interfering with his telepathic ability.' She shook her head and sighed. 'You two had better go and play quietly in Marcus's room for now.'

As they went upstairs, Marcus wasn't smiling any more.

'Dad really loves his animals,' he said. 'He feels awful if even one of them is hurt. It must be terrible for him to know they're all out there and frightened.'

'But there's nothing that can hurt them,' Pippa said, remembering how empty the streets had been on their way home. 'The newsflash said everyone should stay inside, so the animals won't get hurt by traffic or anything. Anyway, look how well the plan's working. Princess Power and Animo can't do anything! And soon Captain Excelsior won't be able to either.'

'As long as Ben's plan works,' Marcus reminded her. 'He wasn't sure if it would.'

They looked at each other seriously and crossed their fingers. Ben's plan was the most dangerous of all.

When Ben had left his house that morning, he'd waited at the bus stop until his mum had closed the door and then he'd walked in the other direction. He'd talked with the others about how to make his part of the plan work and in the end they'd decided to do something very dangerous.

Ben had to find somewhere to hide—where no one could find him—and in the end they'd all agreed the only place was in Dr D. Void's lair. Even Pippa had looked a bit worried about this.

'I know he's your dad, Jewel,' she said. 'But he is an arch villain.'

'My dad wouldn't hurt him,' Jewel promised. 'And besides, he won't even know Ben's there. He can hide in my room and Toby and I will bring him snacks. He'll be fine.'

All the same, as Ben walked into the multi-storey car park where Jewel had said there was a secret entrance to the underground base, he couldn't help feeling a bit scared. But it was all right, Toby was waiting on level B5, and he grinned as Ben walked up.

'The plan's working brilliantly,' he said. 'I thought I should wait for you here to help you get past the guards.' Leading Ben to a piece of concrete wall just like all the others, he took a remote control out of his pocket and pressed a big red button.

The button went *beep* quietly and then the entire wall lifted up like a garage door to show a long curving silver tunnel on the other side. There were also two fierce-looking men in black uniforms holding guns. Ben swallowed nervously but Toby just sauntered in.

'Hi, Bill. How's it going, Norm,' he said and the guards waved back.

'Morning, Toby,' Norm said. 'Everything's very quiet here. Bill and I were about to have our tea break.'

'This is my friend Ben,' Toby told them. 'His mum works for Doctor D. Void. He's come round to practise karate with me.'

'Nice to meet you, Ben,' Bill said, shaking his hand. 'So, who's your mum then?'

Ben gulped and wondered if he should make something up.

'She's the Fade,' Toby said quickly and then hurried Ben into the silver tunnel before the guards asked any more difficult questions. 'Sorry about that,' he whispered once they were out of earshot. 'Everyone knows everyone else here.'

'What if this Fade person comes in though?' Ben said, worriedly. 'Won't they ask her about her kid?'

'No, no, that won't happen,' Toby assured him. 'The Fade's invisible. No one ever sees her so they won't be asking her anything. Besides, she does have a kid, I think. She's always asking me what a boy my age likes to eat or do or play with.'

'Oh, I see.' Ben realized how much of this Toby had planned out. 'That's clever.'

'Now all we have to do is hide you in Jewel's room,' Toby told him. 'She had to go to school this morning or the doctor would have got suspicious. But she'll be back this afternoon.' He grinned at Ben. 'It's going to be cool having you here,' he said. 'I get so bored during the day while Jewel's off having fun.'

'School's not fun!' Ben said, surprised. 'I hate it there. No one ever picks me for teams or sits with me at lunch.'

'If I went to your school, I would,' Toby said. 'But I'm not supposed to need to know anything

 except how to shoot things or hit things or push big red buttons marked "push".'

As he hustled Ben through the black corridors,

Toby filled him in on how the plan was going.

'I've been watching the news,' he said. 'The mayor is furious and the Hero Squad are nowhere to be seen. People are starting to wonder if they've turned evil!'

5
Summing Up

When Captain Excelsior and Princess Power got back to Hero Heights they found Animo sitting slouched in a chair with a miserable expression.

'Someone's out to get us,' he told them. 'They sabotaged the Princess Power dolls and destroyed the city zoo and my Menagerie. Animals are running loose all over the city and I can't get any of them to listen to me.'

'It has to be an evil plot,' the princess agreed. 'I can't understand how anyone managed to reprogram the dolls and my robots, but they're causing chaos all over the city.'

She punched some buttons on the computer and got it to display a big map of Multiplicity with the positions of the destructive dolls and rampaging robots pinpointed with pink dots.

'It's always an evil plot,' Captain Excelsior agreed. 'But we still don't know who did this. We need more information.'

He looked over at the princess to ask her a question and saw that she had turned pale. Looking back at him, she said, 'Captain, I think you had better see this.'

Captain Excelsior came to look at where she was pointing. The computer was showing that they'd received an email message from an unknown source. They watched as the princess displayed it for them.

ATTENTION—HERO SQUAD!

THE ROBOT ARMY HAS KIDNAPPED A BOY FROM BOLD AND BRAVE JUNIOR SCHOOL.

HE WILL BE DROPPED INTO A GIANT VAT OF PINK ACID UNLESS CAPTAIN EXCELSIOR

PROMISES TO QUIT THE SUPER HERO BUSINESS
BY MIDNIGHT TONIGHT.

Captain Excelsior went pale and the other super heroes looked at him with concern.

'Oh no,' Princess Power said. 'It looks as if the villains are going for you next, Captain.'

'You don't understand,' the captain said, already heading for the open window. 'My son goes to that school . . .'

'You have a son?' Animo asked, surprised that he'd never heard of the captain having a family.

But Excelsior was gone. He'd leapt out on to the windowsill as Animo was speaking and was already a distant speck of gold in the sky.

While the Hero Squad were wondering who was responsible for their problems, Dr D. Void was blaming them all for his. He'd watched the midday newsflash and it had made him so angry that by the time Jewel got home from school, he was still in the middle of a massive tantrum.

'How dare they turn evil!' he shouted. 'I'm the evil one! Me, me, me! I've been trying to destroy this city for years and now they switch sides on me . . .' He threw his adjustable spanner across the room and it smashed into the partly built catapult with a shattering noise. 'Shooting into space is too good for them!'

The henchmen and assistant villains were standing around awkwardly, shifting their feet and talking in whispers. Most of them were thinking that the Hero Squad seemed to be making a better job of being evil than Dr D. Void ever had. A few were even wondering about changing sides. The rest were trying to brush cat hair off their uniforms and wondering if they'd be paid danger money if the doctor didn't calm down.

Jewel crept quietly past and along the tunnels to her bedroom. Even though the door was shut she could hear voices from inside and when she opened it Ben and Toby turned round from the video game they'd been playing.

'Aww, Jewel. You made me miss the bonus,' Toby complained, turning back and pressing buttons quickly on his controller.

'Don't mind me,' Jewel said. 'It's only my room, after all.'

Ben had already put his controller down and was looking up at her with a smile.

'The plan's been going really well,' he said. 'Marcus and Pippa called to say all the animals are gone from Animo's zoo and it's chaos at Power Towers.'

'And we sent the kidnap message just ten minutes ago,' Toby added as the video game ended and the screen said 'You Win'.

'Dad seems pretty annoyed as well,' Jewel told them. 'He really believes the Hero Squad have turned evil.'

'Everyone believes it,' Toby said proudly. 'I wouldn't be surprised if even Captain Excelsior had doubts. One thing's certain, no one's going to want super heroes now!'

'And if there are no heroes there'll be no need for villains, either,' Jewel beamed. 'Dad wouldn't invent half as many evil schemes if he wasn't always trying to beat the Hero Squad.'

Captain Excelsior had landed at Bold and Brave Junior School and had gone straight to see the head teacher. He was still hoping it was all a big mistake but when he showed the Head the message, she looked worried.

'We are missing one student,' she said. 'Ben Carter didn't come into school today.' She frowned. 'To be honest we weren't that surprised. Ben's been absent from school before, especially on Mondays.'

'What? Why Mondays?' the captain demanded and the head teacher sighed sadly.

'Ben doesn't get on well with his father,' she said. 'His parents are divorced and Ben always seems unhappy after spending a weekend at his father's flat.'

'He does?' Captain Excelsior looked horrified. 'I had no idea.'

'How could you?' the Head said. 'Even you can't be expected to know if one little boy isn't very happy. I think the real problem is that Ben's father isn't very involved in his life. Ben's always the last child to be collected from school and when he writes about what he did at the weekend it's always about how his father has cancelled plans to spend time with him.'

Captain Excelsior said nothing. He had never realized before how often he had left Ben alone while saving Multiplicity. Maybe Captain Excelsior couldn't look after every little boy but Keith Carter ought to pay more attention to his own son.

'I'll save Ben,' he told the Head. 'Whatever it takes.'

But as he left the school he was wondering what he could possibly do. The robots had demanded he give up being a hero. But if he did that he had no way of knowing if they'd give Ben back. His only hope was to find his son before midnight tonight.

Flying back over the city he tried to think of a plan but it was hard to concentrate. He didn't feel like Captain Excelsior the hero any more but like Keith Carter, deadbeat dad. Instead of flying back to Hero Heights he stopped on the roof of his apartment building and changed back into normal clothes before going inside.

His girlfriend, Fay, was in the living room and when she saw him she looked worried.

'What's wrong, Keith?' she asked. 'You look terrible.' She wasn't speaking with her usual bouncy exclamation marks.

'The pink robot army has kidnapped Ben,' Keith said. 'They're demanding Captain Excelsior give up being a hero for ever if we want to get him back.' Too late he remembered that Keith Carter wouldn't know that. But Fay seemed not to have noticed.

'That's terrible,' she was saying. 'There's got to be something we can do.'

'I don't know,' Keith said, putting his head in his hands. 'I can't think of anything.'

Princess Power and Animo hadn't thought of any good ideas either but they also hadn't given up.

'I'm going to try and persuade the robots to see reason,' she said. 'If they're kidnapping children now, things have gone way too far. I have to find some way to stop them.'

'You can't go out there dressed like that,' Animo pointed out. 'You said the captain nearly shot you once already.'

'You're right,' the princess agreed. 'And to be honest, I'm sick of the sight of pink. I'll go and change and you'll have to look after things here. Perhaps you can use the Etheric Oscillator to broadcast an interference beam.'

'The what?' Animo asked and the princess rolled her eyes.

'The Etheric Oscillator,' she said. 'We got it from that mad scientist last month, remember? It sends out a wave of static that interferes with robotic programming. But you have to direct it right or every computer in the city will crash.'

She zipped out of the room before Animo had time to say anything else and he looked around at the complicated computers that surrounded him. He had no idea how they worked, he couldn't even programme a DVD player by himself. He'd always thought computers were a waste of time but now he felt like an idiot for not having listened when his own son was telling him about them.

Thank goodness Marcus is all right, he thought. He realized how bad Captain Excelsior must be feeling and looked at the computers again. He'd got to find a way to make them work. If he didn't, the captain's own son would be drowned in pink acid!

Pippa and Marcus were watching the news. They weren't smiling any more. It looked as if the plan had worked almost too well.

'. . . there has been no sign of the missing Princess Power dolls since their attack on the Menagerie. However, the pink robots are still destroying the city and although people have been warned to stay off the streets a number of animals have been hurt,' the report announced, over pictures of destroyed buildings and a crowd of people running away.

'Dad's animals!' Marcus gasped, jumping to his feet.

'News just in from Power Towers seems to show that Princess Power may be about to lead the rest of the robots to join them.'

On the television screen there was a picture of Poppet and the other pink robots waving weapons threateningly while a figure flew down from the sky towards them. Princess Power had abandoned her usual pink costume and was wearing a bright red leather flying suit and her golden hair was hidden underneath a red flying cap.

'Is that really Mum?' Pippa said, staring, and then jumping up to join Marcus. 'She's not going to lead the robots, she's going to try and make them stop. What if they don't recognize her in that costume?'

'It's all going wrong,' Marcus realized. 'We have to call Toby and the others.'

But just then Melissa Mondrian came into the room carrying a mobile phone.

'Marcus,' she said. 'It's your father. He wants to speak to you.'

At Doctor D. Void's lair, the others had realized themselves that there was a problem. When they'd heard the robots had hurt some of the animals Jewel had looked alarmed.

'Those poor creatures,' she said. 'Toby, signal the robots and send them in another direction.'

'I can't,' said Toby awkwardly. 'There's no off switch for the rampage program. They're just supposed to keep destroying stuff until their batteries run down or someone shows up to stop them. Generally the Hero Squad manage it sooner or later.'

'The Hero Squad can't help!' Ben pointed out. 'Not this time. No one's going to stop the rampage. And it's all our fault.'

'It's my fault,' Toby said. 'Using the program was my idea but I didn't think it through. I guess it's not as easy as I thought to come up with a foolproof plan.'

'Maybe Dad's invented something that can help,' Jewel said. 'Quick, to the lab!'

They ran out of Jewel's room and along the silver tunnels to Dr D. Void's experimental lab. To Jewel's surprise there was no sound of ranting or raving. Instead, all the henchmen were busily working away at a new invention. Dr D. Void was humming happily to himself as he wired a panel of complicated circuitry.

'Dad,' Jewel said, coming up to him. 'About those robots that are rampaging about the city . . .'

'Oh, that,' the doctor said. 'It's obvious my cunning plans are wasted on Multiplicity, especially if everyone can get so worked up about such stupid-looking robots. If the Hero Squad have turned evil, good luck to them. I've decided to concentrate on something much more important.'

'What is it?' Ben asked, forgetting he wasn't supposed to be here.

'It's a spaceship,' Toby said, before the doctor could answer, looking in awe at the pieces of equipment filling the room.

'That's right,' Dr D. Void agreed. 'I had this wonderful plan to shoot Captain Excelsior into space and then I thought that actually space sounds rather interesting. So I decided to take a vacation from villainy. Once the ship is built I'll be going on a tour of the solar system. Tench and the others can look after the lair while I'm gone.'

The doctor started humming again as he went back to work on the machinery; he seemed to have forgotten they were there.

'I guess you got what you wanted, Jewel,' Ben said, trying to be pleased for her. 'You too, Toby.'

His eyes were stinging and he thought he

might be about to cry. Turning away so the others wouldn't see, he found himself walking into someone.

'Hello, Ben,' a voice said quietly.

Melissa Mondrian drove Marcus and Pippa to Hero Heights in her car.

'I can't believe Dad's actually asked for my help with the computers,' Marcus whispered to Pippa. 'He even said he was sorry he hadn't paid more attention to me before.'

'I'm worried about my mum,' Pippa whispered back. 'I don't care about the plan any more. We've got to stop the robots if we can.'

When they got to Hero Heights, Animo was there to meet them and he gave Marcus a tight hug.

'You have to help me with these computers,' he said. 'Princess Power thought of a way to interfere with the robots' programming using the Etheric Oscillator but I don't know how to make it work!'

'All right, Dad, calm down,' Marcus said reassuringly. But as he looked around at the complicated computers he crossed his fingers. 'The first thing we've got to do is find the manual,' he explained. 'That should tell us how to work the Oscillator.'

'This could take ages,' Pippa said. 'I'm going to make a telephone call. I've got an idea of my own.'

Marcus didn't waste time asking her what her plan was. He was already sitting down at the computer chair and trying to work out the controls. Meanwhile Pippa had gone to find Princess Power's room. It wasn't hard. Of all the rooms in Hero Heights it was the only one with a pink door. Inside, everything was pink too, including the discarded uniform lying over the arm of a chair.

Pippa picked it up and made a face. She'd never thought it would come to this. But she had to get Poppet's attention and she knew only one sure way of doing that. With difficulty she struggled into the pink suit and went to the video phone. Turning it on she pressed the buttons for Power Towers and watched while the fluffy pink shape of Poppet appeared on the screen.

'Poppet,' she said. 'This is Pippa Power. It's very important that you listen to me.'

'Hi there, Pipsqueak!' Poppet said chirpily. 'Oooh, don't you look pretty? What can I do for you?'

'Remember that present I gave you last night?' Pippa asked. 'That special hug program? Well, there's something a bit wrong with it . . .'

Back at Dr D. Void's secret lair, Ben was staring at the patch of nothing he'd walked into.

'Hello?' he said uncertainly. 'Who's there?'

'The doctor calls me the Fade,' a voice said quietly. 'What are you doing here, Ben? Your father thinks the robots kidnapped you.'

'It was a plan,' Ben admitted. 'But it's all gone wrong.'

'Why don't you tell me about it,' the Fade said gently. 'And I'll help you if I can.'

Something in her voice made Ben feel that she really did care about him and he did his best to explain the Super Zeroes and the plan they'd made to get back at their parents, so that they would behave like ordinary grown-ups.

'Heroes and villains just cause trouble for everyone,' he told her. 'They think they're so special and they don't care about normal people at all.'

'Did you think about normal people when you were making your plan?' the Fade asked him. 'Or were you just trying to get back at your father for being too busy to spend time with you?'

'All I wanted was for Dad to care about me,' Ben said, looking down at his feet. 'I didn't want anyone to get hurt.'

'Your father cares about you, Ben,' the woman's voice said and he felt her put an arm around his shoulders. 'But sometimes, even when you know someone really well, you don't properly see them.'

Ben looked up. The space wasn't empty any more. Instead there was a woman dressed in plain grey overalls; she had serious brown eyes and her red hair was tied back in a long plait.

'Fay!' Ben gasped, recognizing his dad's girlfriend. 'You're the Fade?'

'You're not the only one who has friends on both sides,' Fay said smiling at him. 'And your dad's not the only one with a secret identity.'

'You knew about it all the time,' Ben realized. 'You must be a really good actress.'

'Thank you!' Fay exclaimed, putting on her bouncy cheerleader voice for a moment. Then she looked serious again. 'But it's not an act that I care about you and your dad and I think the two of you need to talk. Will you come back home with me?'

That evening there was another newsflash and this time the newsreader looked a bit embarrassed.

'This evening the robot rampage was brought to a quick end when the Hero Squad used an Etheric Oscillator to interfere with the robots' programming,' he said. *'At Power Towers, the rest of the pink robots laid down their weapons and surrendered to Princess Power. It's now believed that their strange behaviour was due to a computer virus. The princess has apologized to anyone whose property was damaged today and has promised to pay for all rebuilding costs.'*

There was a picture of Princess Power handing over a giant cheque to the mayor. She was still wearing a red jumpsuit and the cheque was plain white, signed in black ink.

'*In related news, the super hero Animo has successfully recaptured all the animals from the city zoo and his own Menagerie. In a statement received earlier today he said that he couldn't have done it without the help of the zookeepers and animal welfare experts who used tranquillizer darts to subdue the animals so that they could hear the hero's telepathic commands.*'

This time the pictures were of the animals being brought back to Animo's zoo while the super hero greeted each one with a pat or a stroke.

'*It seems clear now that the Hero Squad have worked as hard as always to protect the city from an extraordinarily cunning plan,*' the newsreader went on. '*We wanted Captain Excelsior to comment but unfortunately were unable to contact him. Staff at Hero Heights said that the captain is spending this evening with his family and explained that even super heroes sometimes need time off.*'

The reporter smiled and shuffled his papers before going on.

'*In other news a scientist, Doctor Damian Void, today unveiled plans to build a spaceship which will produce the first complete map of the solar system. We now go to a full report from our Science Expert . . .'*

Ben watched the news report at his dad's flat. Everyone had been so relieved to have him back that they hadn't asked awkward questions when he and Fay arrived home. Keith Carter had ordered Ben's favourite kind of Indian take-away to celebrate.

Later, once they'd finished eating and Fay was showing Ben's mum her ideas for repainting Ben's room, Ben and his dad had a long talk.

'I was so worried about you today,' Keith began.

'I know, Dad,' Ben said. 'And I should tell you something . . .'

'Let me tell you something first,' Keith said. 'I visited your school and some things the head teacher said made me see that I haven't been a very good dad. I've been so wrapped up in my work that I haven't spent enough time with you.'

'That's OK,' Ben said but his dad shook his head.

'It isn't OK,' he said. 'And I'll try to be better. But there's something I need to tell you about me. It's not an excuse for the way I've been acting, but I hope it'll help you understand. The thing is, Ben, I'm a super hero.'

Ben smiled and said, 'Don't worry, Dad. I forgive you.'

Later, when they were all playing a board game and drinking hot chocolate, Ben excused himself for a minute. Going to his room he took out the video phone his dad had given him last Christmas and called the other Zeroes.

'That's great, Ben,' Jewel said when he'd told them what had happened. She was in her room packing a suitcase. 'And it's cool that you've got a video phone. We can call each other even when I'm in space with my father.'

'While the doctor's gone my dad's going to be running the secret lair,' Toby added. 'And I'm going to ask him if I can come to your school.'

'Mum says she's sick of pink,' Pippa added with a grin. 'And of Princess Power dolls. She's closing the toy company and she's hired decorators to repaint the palace. Although I think it would be easier to knock the whole thing down and start again.'

'Dad said he was really proud of me for figuring out how the Oscillator worked,' Marcus told them. 'He's asked me to teach him how to use a computer properly.'

'That's all great,' Ben said, relieved. 'You know, even though the plan went wrong at the end, I enjoyed making it up. I think I understand now why heroes and villains are always battling each other. Making plans is fun.'

'Well, next time we'll do better,' Toby said.

'Next time?' Jewel asked. 'Didn't we cause enough trouble this time?'

'It's fun being a villain,' Pippa admitted. 'As long as no one gets hurt.'

'It's not so bad being a hero, either,' Marcus agreed. 'As long as we have a good leader.'

They all looked at Ben from the four quarters of the video screen and he grinned back at them all.

'You know,' he said. 'I never did tell my dad about the Super Zeroes. Everything worked out so well in the end that I didn't want to worry him. I guess that means we're still a team.'

'But what kind of team?' Pippa asked. 'Are we heroes or villains or normal people?'

'We're friends,' Ben said. 'Isn't that what we made the team for in the first place, really? To help each other? So the next time any of us needs help . . .'

'Super Zeroes to the rescue!' Toby announced.